One day, the time came for him to tell his parents . . .

. . . he wanted to be
an astronaut instead.

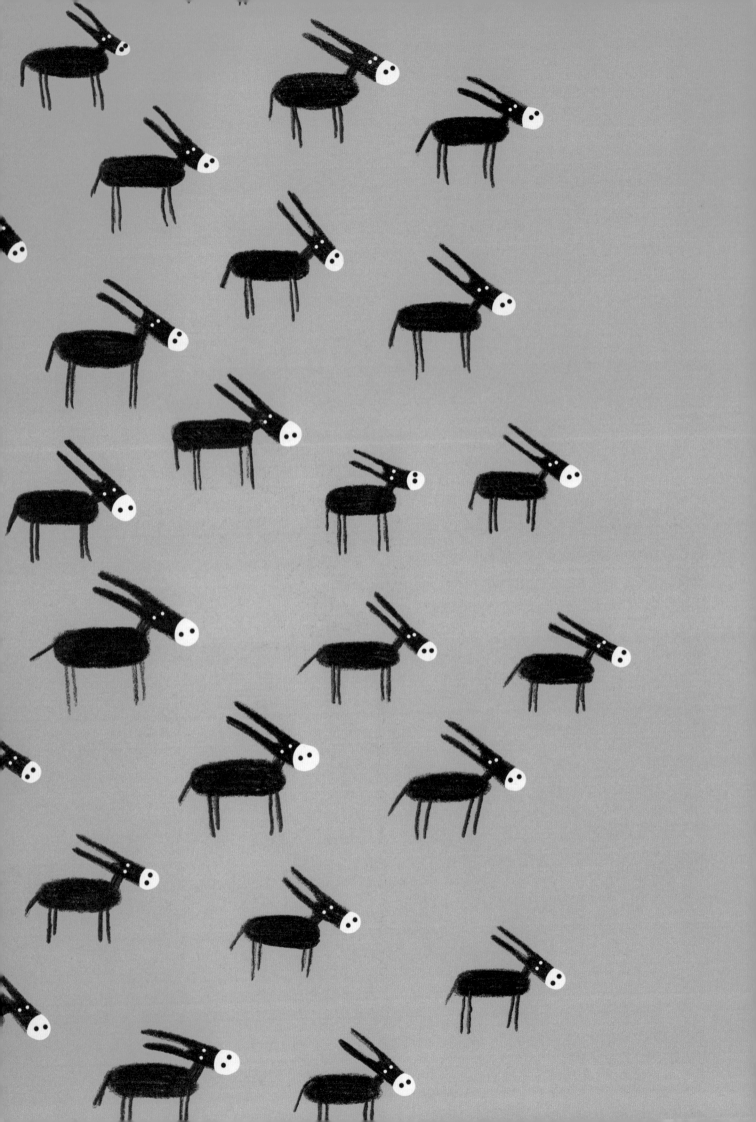

The next morning,
Toto left for the big city.

He was going to find work
and save up for space school.

He promised he would
return as an astronaut.

A few days later, Toto arrived.

At first, he was afraid of the big city.

He felt lonely.
And very small.

Toto missed his family,
but he knew he had to follow his dream.

To save money for space school,
Toto got a job fixing umbrellas.

But when he had just enough money,
some thieves stole all his savings.

The thieves told him that
donkeys could never be astronauts.

Toto felt smaller than ever.

For the first time, he thought about
giving up his dream and going home.

But the next day as Toto went to work,
he met a family.

He told them all about what had happened.
They showed him kindness and love.

Like Toto, the mother had dreamed
of becoming an astronaut too.

She gave Toto her old spacesuit,
and she helped him get to space school.

She told Toto not to give up on
his dreams like she had done.

It gave him the courage to continue.

Back in the village,
Toto's parents grew even sadder.

Would Toto ever come back?

But that night, a loud
sound awoke them . . .

It was a rocket!

Toto had returned, just like he promised.

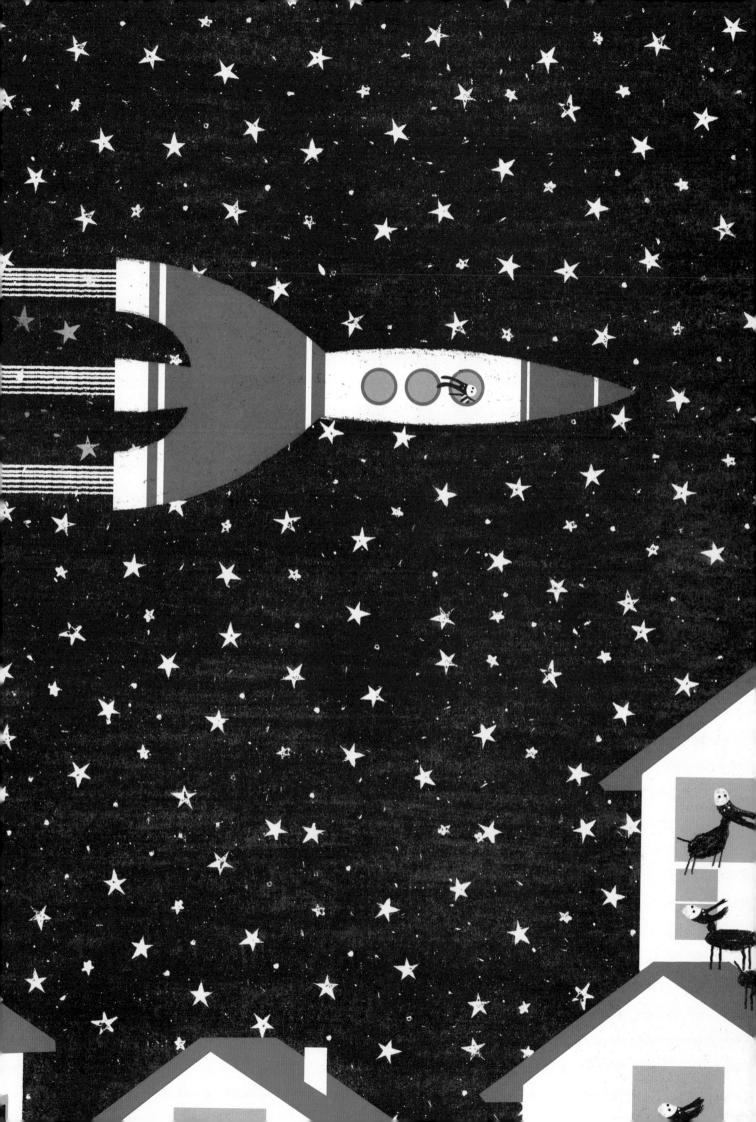

Toto the astronaut took his friends and family somewhere they had never been before.

And that night, the moon was filled with donkeys.

For Olga and Mambo

A TEMPLAR BOOK

First published in the UK in 2018 by Templar Publishing,
an imprint of Kings Road Publishing, part of Bonnier Books UK,
The Plaza, 535 King's Road, London, SW10 0SZ
www.templarco.co.uk
www.bonnierbooks.co.uk

1 3 5 7 9 10 8 6 4 2

ISBN 978-1-78741-153-1

This book was typeset in ITC Avant Garde Gothic.
The illustrations were created with graphite,
wax and ink, and coloured digitally.

Edited by Joanna McInerney
Designed by Olivia Cook and Kieran Hood

Printed in China